Rourke 10-11
15.95

Words to Know Before You Read

brave

cheered

handkerchief

numb

rebound

score

stitches

tied

www.rourkepublishing.com

Edited by Luana Mitten
Illustrated by Sarah Conner
Art Direction and Page Layout by Renee Brady

Library of Congress Cataloging-in-Publication Data

Picou, Lin
 Ouch! Stitches / Lin Picou.
     p. cm. -- (Little Birdie Books)
  ISBN 978-1-61741-819-8 (hard cover) (alk. paper)
  ISBN 978-1-61236-023-2 (soft cover)
 Library of Congress Control Number: 2011924696

Rourke Publishing
Printed in China, Voion Industry
  Guangdong Province
042011
042011LP

www.rourkepublishing.com - rourke@rourkepublishing.com
Post Office Box 643328 Vero Beach, Florida 32964

Ouch! Stitches

Written by Lin Picou

Illustrated by Sarah Conner

Score! Now the game is tied!

Sophia and I were playing basketball with our friends, Jayden and Lily. Lily scored and then Sophia got the ball.

Sophia had a shot at the net, but Jayden blocked her and caught the rebound.

Jayden ran to the center line before tossing the basketball into the air to Lily.

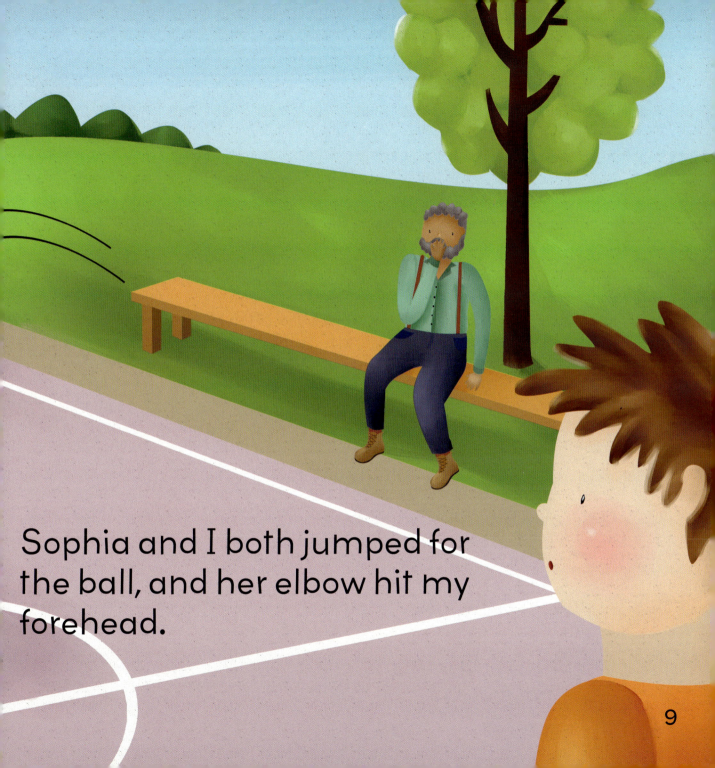

Sophia and I both jumped for the ball, and her elbow hit my forehead.

"Ouch!" There was blood!
Grandpa hurried onto the court
to see if I was OK.

11

12

Grandpa tied a handkerchief around my head to stop the bleeding. Then he said, "We better have a doctor look at this cut."

13

Everyone rode with Grandpa
and me to Dr. Walbur's office. 15

Inside the doctor's office, the nurse cleaned my cut. I was brave and didn't cry.

"You will need a shot to numb the skin around the cut," the doctor told me.

17

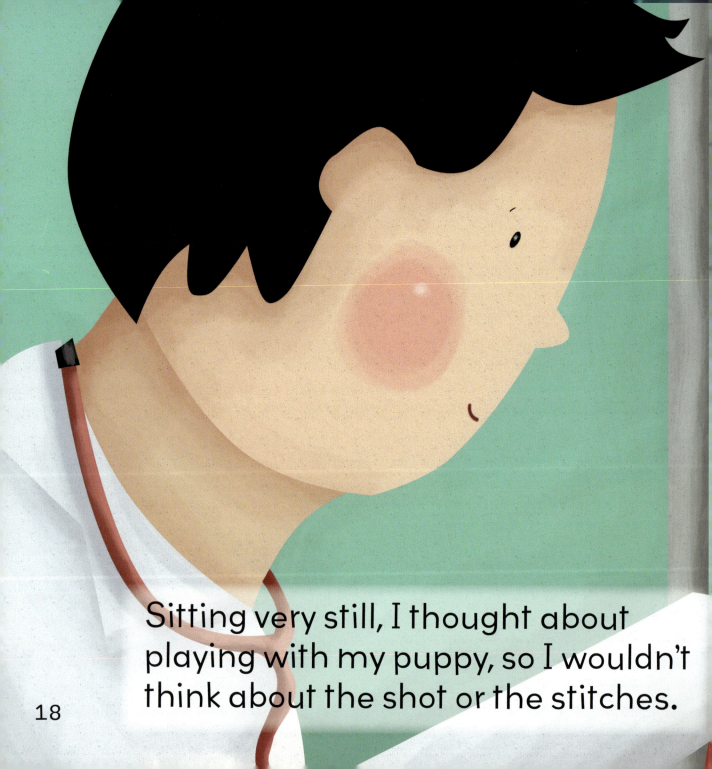

Sitting very still, I thought about playing with my puppy, so I wouldn't think about the shot or the stitches.

"All done!" said Grandpa Ben. "You can open your eyes now."

"Wait a minute!" Dr. Walburn smiled. "I think we need some stitches in those pants, too!"

I looked at my knee and saw that I'd torn a big hole in my jeans. "That can wait until we get home!" I said.

After Reading Activities

You and the Story...

Why did Jayden have to go to the doctor?

What happened at the doctor's office?

Have you ever been injured when playing a game?

Words You Know Now...

Choose three words from the list below. On a piece of paper use those three words to write sentences to start your own story.

brave	rebound
cheered	score
handkerchief	stitches
numb	tied

You Could...Plan a Game with Friends

- What game would you like to play?

- Who will you invite to play with you?

- Make a list of the rules for your game.

- What do you need to play your game?

- Decide when and where you will play your game.

- Invite your friends to join you.

About the Author

Lin Picou rides her bicycle in Land O' Lakes, Florida for exercise. She plays Red Light, Green Light with her students when she's not teaching them reading, writing, or science lessons.

About the Illustrator

Sarah Conner is an illustrator living in London with her cat Berni. When she's not at her drawing-board (or computer!), she enjoys taking walks in London's beautiful parks, having picnics, knitting and gardening.